For my goddaughter, Harmoni.
Stay a princess as long as you can.

Originally published in 2014 by CreateSpace Independent Publishing Platform in the United States of America

No part of this publication may be reproduced, stored in a retrieval system, or
transmitted in any form or by any means, electronic, mechanical, photocopying,
recording, or otherwise, without written permission of the publisher.
For information regarding permission, write to Little, Brown Books for Young Readers,
a division of Hachette Book Group, Inc., 1290 Avenue of the Americas, New York, NY 10104.

ISBN 978-1-338-54803-7

12 11 10 9 8 7   21 22 23 24

Printed in the U.S.A.   40

First Scholastic printing, February 2019

The illustrations for this book were created using watercolor and ink and were digitally finished.
This book was edited by Kheryn Callender and designed by Jamie W. Yee with art direction by Saho Fujii.
The text was set in Barthowheel, and the display type was hand-lettered.

PRINCESS HAIR

BY SHAREE MILLER

SCHOLASTIC INC.

All princesses wear crowns,

but underneath their crowns, not
all princesses have the same hair.

Some princesses wear **PUFFS** and play pretend.

Others wear **TWIST OUTS** and twirl around.

Princesses with **DREADLOCKS** love

to draw
and draw
and draw.

Princesses with KINKS love to think!

And princesses with

FROHAWKS rock!

Princesses with

HEAD
WRAPS

take long naps.

Princesses with CURLS wear pearls.

And princesses with
TEENY-WEENY AFROS
wear teeny-weeny bows.

Princesses with **BANTU KNOTS** bake a LOT!

Princesses with **AFROS** do-si-do.

Princesses with BRAIDS throw parades!

Princesses with **BUNS** love to run.

Princesses with
BLOWOUTS

bounce and bounce and bounce.

Princesses with **TWISTS** wrap gifts.

And NAPPY princesses are HAPPY princesses.

Not every Princess has the same hair.

But every Princess **LOVES** her Princess hair!